A TEMPLAR BOOK

First published in hardback in the UK in 2015
by Templar Publishing, an imprint of The Templar Company Limited,
Deepdene Lodge, Deepdene Avenue, Dorking, Surrey, RH5 4AT
Copyright © 2015 by Levi Pinfold
First edition
All rights reserved
ISBN 978-1-78370-055-4
Edited by Alison Ritchie
Designed by Mike Jolley
Printed in China

GREENLING by LEVI PINFOLD

templar publishing

What is this growing on Barleycorn land?

What is this standing, where once stood a tree?

Is it intended for Barleycorn hands?

I wonder, thinks he, could this be for me?

His wife wants to know where it came from.

He says, "Where the wildflowers grow."

She says, "It belongs to the wild then,

and back to the land it should go."

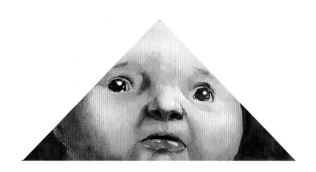

You cannot return for a refund.

A baby is not like a hat.

What's picked is picked, what's done is done,

and that, Barleycorns, is that.

So forget what you know about baby demands.

This is a different breed.

It's clear he has needs only trees understand;

a vegetable hunger to feed.

With night fast approaching Barleycorn says,

"We can't leave him outside for the crows.

If some of this outside were inside,

he could settle in safe, if he chose."

"I know what you're up to," mutters his wife,

"but keeping him here is not right.

Get rid of this goblin by morning.

He goes, or we're in for a fight."

But morning brings stranger becomings, beginning a Barleycorn gripe.

She says, "How will we cook breakfast today?" He says, "Them melons look ripe."

She retreats to the lounge for a lie down, but her hopes of a rest take a blow.

She says, "How will we watch telly tonight?" He says, "Just look at him grow."

Escaping the house is no option, the transport has taken to seed.

She says, "Well there goes the shopping!" He says, "Depends what you need..."

"We've got pumpkins and peppers, spring onions and sage,

apples more golden than money.

Why would we want to pile more on our plate,

when we're already swimming in honey?"

"Dear husband," she says, "what are you? A bee?!

You're beginning to buzz like a drone.

I'm calling for help to fix up your brain."

But grass has invaded the phone.

Retreating in rage to her bedroom,

Mrs Barleycorn goes without tea.

What's clattering there in the night? she thinks.

Why now? Why here? Why me?

A screech of brakes awakes her at dawn, then humming upon the lines…

A swarm of passengers bound for work, are stopped in their tracks by vines.

"This cuckoo must go!" says a voice in the crowd.
"He's pushing us out of our world!
These people all need to be moving along,
the vegetable must be hurled."

That's a bit much, Mrs. Barleycorn thinks,
the boy is just strange, not bad...
A baby's a baby, when all's said and done,
there's no need for them to get mad.

Thoughts boiling over, she bellows aloud,
"Well I think your head's gone wrong.
We should welcome this Greenling into our house,
we've been living in his all along!"

Suddenly flowering with all the attention,

Greenling sits up and speaks;

an old magic word, long since forgotten,

cast an odd spell for weeks...

They ate up the apples, the mangoes and plums, they ate up the oranges too.

They ate up the fruit of the Greenling, fruit much too good to be true.

So a long summer began and continued:
a harvest with each morning light.
Strange and enchanted Greenling cuisine
had everyone hooked on delight.

But all summer things must come to an end,
when summer has grown a beard.
As autumn arrives, the Barleycorns find
that Greenling has disappeared.

Barleycorn says, "He's a Greenling.
Who can say what they intend?
He left us with this for the winter,
but I don't think this is the end..."

What do the hills and the trees have planned?

Does Mr. Barleycorn quite understand?

When winter has passed, and spring is to hand...

What will be growing on Barleycorn land?